# Sunny and Tug
# Go to the Beach

A Children's Story

By

Krista Doyle

Illustrated by Amanda Marsh

To the Little Ones


May you find your voice
and
May you always know that

You are Special
You are Unique
You are Loved

One bright, sunshine-y morning, Sunny's mom walked into the room. She said, "Sunny! Tug! It's such a beautiful day- who wants to go to the beach?

Sunny jumped up and spun in a circle. "The beach! The beach! I love going to the beach!!" Tug looked at her and said, "What's the beach?" He had never been to a beach or the ocean before, so he didn't know why she was so happy.

"The beach is wonderful!", she told him. "There is sand to play on and water to splash in, and it is just so much FUN!"
Tug started to get excited too. "I want to go to the beach, too!"
"Let's go!" their mom said as the dogs ran to get in the car.

As they headed down the highway, Sunny put her head out of the window and remembered all the good times she had at the ocean. But this time was even better because Tug was going too! She couldn't wait to show him all the fun things to do. Soon she could smell the salt water in the air and she knew they were getting close.

The ocean! The oceun! Sunny could see it now- the white sand and the sparkling blue water! She jumped out of the car and headed for the beach. Tug ran up beside her and they raced to see who could get there first.  It was a tie!

They ran to the edge of the water and Sunny showed Tug how to jump the little waves before they came up on the sand. It was so much fun and they played and played. After a while, they thought it was time for a snack.  (Sunny and Tug were always ready for a yummy treat). Then they stretched out on the cool sand under the umbrella and took a nap.

"Ahhh! That was such a great nap! Let's go for a walk, Tug!", Sunny said. Of course Tug wanted to go anywhere with Sunny. They were best friends!

Soon they were walking on a little path that led to a small park. "Look, Sunny!", Tug exclaimed. "What IS that over there?"

Sunny looked over and saw the biggest, hairiest dog she had ever seen. "Let's go see!", she said to Tug.

As they got closer to the dog, suddenly he saw them and ran towards them. Tug was a little afraid, because he didn't know if the dog was friendly. Then the dog opened his mouth and said very softly, "**woof**! Hi there! My name is Harry! What's yours?"

Tug couldn't believe that such a big dog had such a soft voice! He liked Harry right away, and stepped right up to him and said, "Hi Harry! I'm Tug and this is Sunny! Do you want to come play with us?"

"Sure! I'd love to!", Harry said and the three dogs started back down the path. Sunny and Tug were so happy that they had a new friend to have fun with at the beach.

When they got back to the umbrella, they got a drink of water. Then they were ready to go into the ocean! "Ok," their mom said. "But don't go out too far. The currents in the ocean are strong and they will carry you away from the beach."

Tug wasn't sure what that meant, but Sunny seemed to understand and soon they were swimming in the ocean! Harry didn't swim, because his hair was so long. He decided to stay on the beach and watch Sunny and Tug have fun.

After a while, Sunny looked towards the beach and she couldn't see anything she knew. But she knew she had to be brave for Tug, so she told him, "We'll make it back soon!". She started swimming very hard, but she wasn't sure where to go, and soon she started to get tired.

*Tug looked, and the beach seemed so far away! "Sunny! Sunny!*

*Look how far out in the ocean we are!" He began to get a little scared,*

*because he couldn't see where the umbrella was, or their mom, or even Harry.*

Then all of a sudden, she heard a sound. It was a woof! She looked around and she didn't see anything. But then she heard it again! Woof! It was so soft – if she could just see where it was coming from!

In the very next moment, she heard the most beautiful sound—it was a BIG "**WOOF**"!! She looked and there was Harry! Then she knew exactly where they had to swim, and she said, "C'mon Tug! Over here!" She was so happy to see Harry.  They swam as hard as they could and soon they were on the sand.

*"Harry! Harry! We are so happy to see you! Thank you for your big, wonderful WOOF!", Sunny said. "But we thought you had such a quiet voice!"*

*Harry said, "So did I! I never knew that I had such a big voice until I met you and Tug, and I just had to help you! I could see you but I couldn't tell you that you were going too far out in the ocean. I tried to warn you, but you couldn't hear me! Then all of a sudden, I felt this big **WOOF** coming out of my mouth and I was so happy!"*

*"We were happy, too!", Sunny said.*

*The three dogs jumped up and down with joy. Harry even did some spins in a circle, saying "WOOF! WOOF! WOOF!" Sunny and Tug laughed with him. They were so happy to hear his big voice!*

*Suddenly Sunny stopped and said, "We better get back to Mom! She is probably worried about us!"*
*They all started running on the sand towards the umbrella and their mom. They were so glad to see her!*

Soon it was time to say goodbye to their new friend, Harry. It had been such a fun day and Sunny and Tug knew that they would never forget him, or how he had helped them.

As they drove away, Sunny and Tug shouted out the window, "Good bye, Harry! We will miss you! Don't ever forget that you have that big, beautiful voice inside of you!!!"

And Harry said,

## "WOOF!"

Made in the USA
Columbia, SC
17 November 2024

46660827R00018